Happy Birthday, Jamie!

Love, Aunt Kelley, Uncle Weston, & Baby T

BABAR

VISITS ANOTHER PLANET

LAURENT DE BRUNHOFF

BABAR

VISITS ANOTHER PLANET

Abrams Books for Young Readers, New York

Babar and his family were picnicking outside the city of Celesteville when Cousin Arthur said, "I think I see a rocket ship!"

It *was* a rocket. It landed nearby and sucked them all in—Babar, Celeste, Arthur, the three children, and even Zephir the monkey.

There was no pilot or flight attendant, but a friendly robot offered them cookies and played music. Everyone tried to stay calm.

Safe in the rocket, they passed the moon
and the planet Mars. At last, near an unknown
planet, they felt the rocket slow down.

When they landed and the door opened, Babar climbed down the ladder and put one foot onto a surface like caramel.

"Stop right there!" shouted Arthur. "The rest of you might get stuck, too."

A fleet of skimmercraft approached, piloted by strange-looking creatures. "Come see!" Babar said, abandoning his shoe. "They look like elephants, but they are not elephants!"

The skimmercraft carried them to docking platforms, and
from there they were whisked away by flying eggs.

A city appeared, hanging from enormous red balloons.
It floated above the pale beige surface of the planet.

"It's true," Celeste observed, "that if their houses were on the surface, they might sink."

The egg taxis deposited the elephants on terraces in the floating city. Two officials greeted them, one with a mushroom on his head, the other with a totem pole on his.

Mr. Totem apologized for taking them from home so abruptly. He admitted that he may have been too eager for their visit.

Babar agreed. "But since you meant no harm, we will not hold it against you."

Mr. Totem took them to his house, which had a swimming pool in the living room.

"Truly," said Arthur as he swam with his new friends and Flora played with a blue-spotted puppy, "travel is good for you."

Their beds were cubbies in the wall. The children climbed in quickly, but Babar and Celeste did not fit. Mr. Totem emptied the pool and filled it with pillows for his guests.

In the morning, a breakfast fountain tossed muffins at the elephants and showered them with juice. Drinking the juice took some practice.

Mr. Totem took Babar shopping for shoes, but the biggest pair in the store was not big enough. Eventually Babar took off his remaining shoe and walked in his socks.

The highlight of the day was a tournament. Hundreds of spectators gathered in a stadium to watch contestants ride the eggs and try to unseat one another.

Arthur took part. And bravo! He knocked his opponent off his egg and into the net below! Arthur was so surprised at his victory that he, too, fell off his egg.

He bounced so high that he collided with his own egg and ripped one of the balloons holding the city.
    The crowd was scared and started to run.

That made the platform tilt even more. But Babar and Celeste calmed everyone down and helped them move to a safer platform.

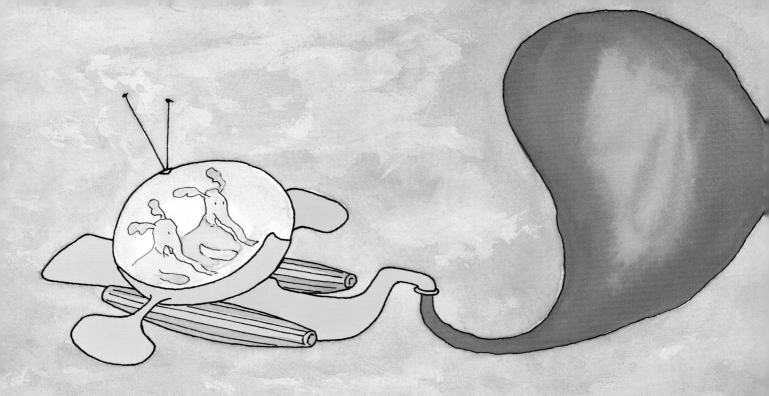

Very soon a rescue crew arrived to replace the damaged balloon. The platform hung safe again. The danger was over.

Arthur had a big bump on his head. It was not serious, but Babar and Celeste thought it might serve as an excuse to leave. "I'd love to get him home to see a doctor," said Celeste.

Mr. Totem was concerned. "Of course you must go home. It was selfish of me to bring you here! There is more I want to show you, but Arthur's health comes first."

Mr. Totem gave Flora the
blue-spotted puppy to
remember their visit. He
and Mr. Mushroom waved
good-bye as the rocket
blasted off into space.

Back in Celesteville, they were welcomed with joy by all their friends, who had been terribly worried about them.

"We have also brought back wonderful memories," said Babar. "We've had a fine adventure. It isn't every day you get taken to another planet."

"I certainly hope not," said their friend the Old Lady.

The artwork for each picture is prepared using watercolor on paper.
This text is set in 16-point Comic Sans.

The Library of Congress has cataloged the original Abrams edition of this book as follows:

Library of Congress Cataloging-in-Publication Data

Brunhoff, Laurent de, 1925–
    [Babar sur la planète molle. English]
    Babar visits another planet / Laurent de Brunhoff.
      p. cm.
Summary: Babar and his family are abducted and taken by rocket ship to an unknown planet
where the residents are very hospitable and there are many interesting sights to see.
    ISBN 0-8109-4244-5
    [1. Elephants—Fiction. 2. Extraterrestrial beings—Fiction. 3. Space flight—Fiction.]   I.
Title.
    PZ7.B82843Babif 2003
    [Fic]—dc21

                                                                          2002009800

ISBN for this edition: 978-1-4197-0342-3

Printed and bound in China
10 9 8 7 6 5 4 3 2 1

Abrams Books for Young Readers are available at special discounts when purchased in quantity
for premiums and promotions as well as fundraising or educational use. Special editions can also
be created to specification. For details, contact specialsales@abramsbooks.com or the address
below.

115 West 18th Street
New York, NY 10011
www.abramsbooks.com